WARREN WEASEL'S
WORSE THAN MEASLES

WARREN WEASEL'S
WORSE THAN MEASLES

BY ALICE BACH

DRAWINGS BY
HILARY KNIGHT

Harper & Row, Publishers

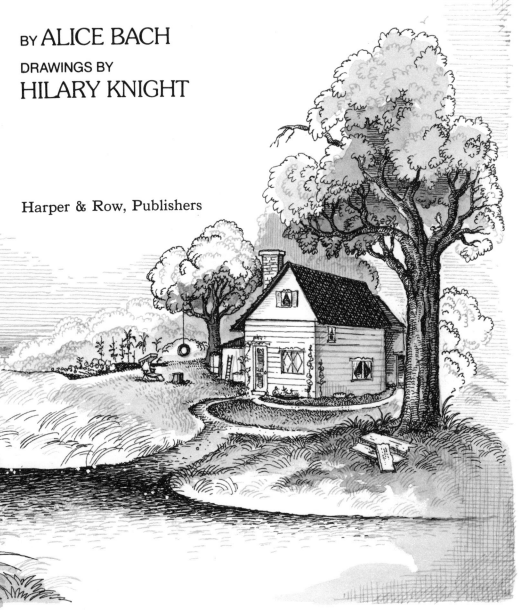

WARREN WEASEL'S WORSE THAN MEASLES
Text copyright © 1980 by Alice Hendricks Bach
Illustrations copyright © 1980 by Hilary Knight
FIRST EDITION

Library of Congress Cataloging in Publication Data
Bach, Alice.
    Warren Weasel's worse than measles.

    SUMMARY: The smartest bear in the world makes a
winner out of a loser weasel.
    [1. Bears—Fiction.   2.   Weasels—Fiction]
I. Knight, Hilary.   II. Title.
PZ7.B1314War 1979   [E]   78-22491
ISBN 0-06-020324-2
ISBN 0-06-020327-7 lib. bdg.

For Michael Babb,
King of the Great Weasels,
and
For Dory Shannon,
who showed me blue trees.

"Where are you going with that can of paint?" Ma asked.

"To paint the oak tree," Ronald said.

Where are you going with that can of paint?" Ma asked as she sprinkled flour on her pastry board and rolled out her piecrust.

"To paint the oak tree," Ronald said.

"I like to see a bear enjoying the fresh air," Ma smiled placidly.

Ronald swung the can as he went outside. Ever since his twin, Oliver, had swirled his green satin cape around himself and waved good-bye from the circus wagon, Ma and Pa had been twice as nice to Ronald. He was allowed to read late into the night. He was allowed to conduct his experiments in his room with the door closed and curtains drawn. They understood he needed to shield his work from possible spies.

Ronald set the paint can down next to the tree and pried up the lid. His plan was proceeding perfectly. A flock of birds *whooshed* into the sky and flew across the meadow. A good sign, Ronald decided. They are giving me the tree. As soon as the creatures of the woods know the blue oak marks the home of the smartest bear in the universe, they will stop by for my advice.

He wouldn't feel lonely anymore.

He dipped his brush into the can and painted as high as he could reach. But there were many patches of rough brown bark on the tree and splotches of blue all over Ronald.

"Anyone can see this tree is blue," Ronald assured himself.

The rest of the day Ronald spent hanging signs. He liked seeing RONALD in big red letters on every sign. Soon he would have plenty of friends. Lately the only questions he had been asked were about Oliver. Was he enjoying the circus? Was he famous yet? Was he ever coming back?

"Time for supper, son," Pa called. "What have you been doing besides painting yourself and that tree?"

"Not a thing," Ronald trickled a stream of honey in the shape of a capital R onto a thick slice of bread.

"After supper you will wash off that mess," Ma said.

"This kind of paint doesn't wash off," Ronald whispered.

"Was that a knock at the door?"

"At suppertime, Ma?" Pa shook his head and helped himself to another ear of corn.

"Was that a knock at the door?" . . . .

Pa shook his head and helped himself to another ear of corn.

"It certainly was a knock." Ma left the table. "Good heavens," she gasped. "There is a *weasel* at the door."

"Is this the home of Mr. Ronald Bear, the smartest bear in the universe, no problem too large, no creature too small?"

"I am Ronald, but the sign says *until dinner-time*. Come back tomorrow."

"I know I am late, but it took me a long time. The sign is so heavy." He sat down and began to weep.

"Let me see that sign," said Pa. He and Ma read the sign several times. Ronald sensed the time for getting his own way was over.

"You are not what I had in mind." Ronald shook his head in disgust. He was expecting bears, and maybe some beautiful birds with bright red feathers, who could tell him about faraway places.

"My name is Warren and my luck has run out."

Ma lifted Warren onto a chair. "Do have a bit of stew."

"Ma is an exceptional cook." Pa smiled at the tiny creature. Even though tears were still dripping from Warren's eyes, his mouth was

The sign reads:

Meet World famous RONA[
the Smartest bear in the univ[
Genius bear will solve all pro[
every day until dinnert[
No problem too L·A·R·G·E / No Cre[
Turn left at blue oak
fee not a f[ ]tor

"Let me see that sign," said Pa.

set in a grin. "Bears are famous for mouth-watering meals and for being nice to visitors," Pa said.

"It must be swell to be a creature everybody likes." Warren began to cry again.

"Good grief, he is too much." Ronald stomped to the door. "Sorry, Weasel, this is not the House of Miracles. I am a scientist, not a magician."

"Not so fast, Mr. Blue-Bear. Your sign says all predicaments." Pa patted Warren's head. "He is most definitely in a predicament."

"Be right back—I am going to look him up." Ronald went to his room for a book. Pa muttered to Ma, "It's time that bear learns he can't pick and choose creatures as if they were berries on a bush!"

Ronald came back reading loudly: " 'Weasel: a carnivorous animal, related to the mink, the ermine, and the polecat, mostly reddish brown, likely to have a white underbelly'— or in the case of Warren, a yellowish cast to the fur. 'Weasels in the north turn white in the winter.' "

"That about covers it." Warren dropped his pointy black snout onto his chest. "Except for the most important part. Weasels have a bad name with the public."

"Weasel: a carnivorous animal related to the mink."

He wrote, "Very small. Very dumb. Prospects dismal."

"Nonsense. Read it for yourself, nothing about antiweasel movements," Ronald snapped. He opened his notebook and began writing. He wrote, "Very small. Very dumb. Prospects dismal."

"Tell us something about your family," Ma said, settling a cushion behind her back.

"I have seventy, eighty brothers and sisters— we don't keep careful count, what with so many weasels coming and going. Weasels are on the move. Scattered families, some probably up north like Ronald said, turning white."

"What made you leave your family?" Pa asked.

"Well, since spring I have been running with twenty, thirty weasels, mostly cousins. And I began thinking, why can't we settle down near nice folks, congenial bears like you, although I didn't know you then." Warren giggled. Ronald groaned and crossed out several sentences in his notebook.

"Then you saw Ronald's sign?" Ma prompted.

Warren grasped the tabletop with his tiny front paws. "Yes. I do so enjoy the company of others. Most weasels are loners, except for Cousin Lillian. She loves parties—she'd cross half a country for a big blast."

"Tell us something about your family," Ma said.

"I have seventy, eighty brothers and sisters" . . .

"There's nothing about parties on my sign," Ronald growled.

"I don't expect parties, but I saw the sign, see, and I said that's for me." He rubbed his wet eyes on his paw. "A famous bear with a blue tree in his yard. Where I come from, we don't have blue trees."

"Trees don't grow that way. I painted it to attract clients," Ronald hissed.

"Your sign made Warren leave his relations." Pa was angry now.

"You always say, 'Help others and you help yourself.' Since Oliver left, I haven't had anyone to help. So I decided to advertise. I thought bears would come. I can solve *bear* problems." Ronald glared at Warren.

"It's not my fault I'm a weasel," Warren said in a squeak.

"Second cousin to a rat, small head, housing very small brain. Only creatures with brains can be winners."

"True, true. I never won anything, I never even came in second." Warren hiccuped and started weeping again. "Are you really the smartest bear—"

"Yes I am. Someday books will say 'Ronald, the bear scientist of the century.' But science doesn't have all the answers."

Warren hiccuped and started weeping again.

Warren's front paws trembled with excitement. "I have come to the right place."

"Science doesn't deal in miracles." Ronald snorted. "Can you imagine the headlines—'Weasel Astronaut Forgets to Land on Moon'? 'General Warren Weasel Shoots His Own Men in Battle'?"

"Signed up to be an ambulance driver once. Didn't get the job."

"Ambulance driver?" Ronald laughed. "You're more like the accident."

"Just keep up that nasty talk—" Pa warned.

"OK. Sorry, Warren. Maybe I can find you a career. We mustn't forget I am the smartest bear. He can sleep in Oliver's room, can't he, Ma?"

"You ever hear of Don's Trailer-Truck Driver's School?" asked Warren. "Stayed on their porch two weeks, night and day, couldn't reach the doorbell. No one came in or out. Two weeks!" Warren snuffled.

"Just as well, honey, tricycles are more your speed." Ma held Warren in the crook of her arm and took him to Oliver's room. Over her shoulder she muttered to Pa, "A weasel in my house, a weeping weasel sleeping in my house.

What will that bear do next?"

"Weasels are by nature wanderers, my dear, we may wake up and find Warren has wandered away during the night."

"No way." Ronald strode toward Oliver's room. "He may be a weasel but he's all I have. You sleep in my room, where I can watch you." Ronald lifted Warren to his shoulder.

"When I was a young weasel, all the creatures shouted, 'Warren Weasel's worse than measles.' Even other weasels wrote it on the blackboard."

"You do balance awfully well." Ronald wished he could think of something nicer. But clearly the weasel was a mess. "Time for bed."

"I don't want to go to bed. It's almost night."

"Now, no funny business. Oliver always went to bed before me."

"It's time to be waking up. Weasels don't sleep at night." Warren clasped his paws around Ronald's ear.

"Then you watch me sleep," Ronald snapped. He got into bed and asked Warren, "Can you read?"

"Of course."

"Well, you can read to me till I fall asleep."

"Can you read?" asked Ronald. *"Of course,"* replied Warren.

"Well, you can read to me till I fall asleep."

"Shall I wake you in the morning?" Warren smoothed Ronald's pillow and dragged the sheet up over the bear's mountainous shoulder.

"Good idea," Ronald said. Warren patted his shoulder and read from *Breeding Mice for Laboratory Experiments* until Ronald fell asleep.

For three days Ronald read about weasels. There were no famous ones. No parachute champions, no doctors, lawyers, ballet dancers. No construction empires, no movie stars, no weasel universities. But Ronald didn't give up. He liked the way the weasel read slowly and softly each night from whatever book Ronald selected. Warren put the toothpaste on Ronald's brush, wiped the crumbs from under his chair, folded his pajamas, gathered up the dirty cups and glasses for Ma so Ronald could proceed with his work.

Ronald woke Warren one afternoon. "We have to find something you excel at; then we will convince creatures they need that. See?"

Warren sighed. "You are the smartest bear."

Warren shot out the door and sprinted past the blue oak, across the meadow, and back to Ronald, who was sitting next to an immense stack of books.

"Stay in one place," he growled.

Warren put the toothpaste on Ronald's brush.

"I'm best when I get up steam."

"So far we know you cannot dance, you cannot sing, tie knots, paint pictures, read a compass, fix clocks, drive a tourist bus, haul firewood, repair small machines. I will read off a list of jobs guaranteed to make you popular with the public. Stop me when you like the sound of one."

"I'm so excited! Finally, the most wanted weasel in the world, Warren Weasel in person." He danced in a circle and tripped over his tail.

"We already know you can't dance. Now, building houses? Negative. Making taffy or jelly apples? Honey cakes? A-one negative! Selling umbrellas?"

"Don't care much for rain."

"Beekeeper, logroller, politician, salesman, spy, cowboy? Stop crying, you dumb weasel. I have plenty more ideas. Cashier, knife sharpener? Knife thrower? Clown? Sorry, that would never work out. Assembly line in a factory?"

"What's a factory?"

Ronald chewed the end of his pencil. "Nurse, baker, what about writing a book? That's easy."

"How is it coming, boys?" Pa set his chair with the fringed top next to Ronald. Warren streaked past them and circled the meadow several times.

"Come back here, you foolish weasel!" Ronald yelled.

Warren slowed down and zigzagged across the meadow toward the bears.

Perhaps delivering mail—he's got the speed, Ronald thought. Warren crawled under Pa's chair and curled up in a small patch of shade.

"You have wonderful speed. You might be the first animal to be in two places at once." Pa chuckled.

"I've solved your problem. Come here."

"Sun hurts my eyes." Warren sighed but came out, nose to the ground. Saying no to Ronald was as sensible as using a dozing crocodile as a footbridge across a swamp.

"I have solved it. The smartest bear triumphs again." Ronald took a deep breath. "You will be a mailman. That is the end of that. On to bigger animals."

"Fourteen of my brothers are mailmen. I went there right off. Special delivery section. But they're not taking on any new weasels."

Ronald kicked a clod of dirt. "I quit."

Pa turned to Warren. "What about Rodent Control?"

Warren streaked past them . . .

and circled the meadow several times.

"They're the glamorous weasels all right."
Warren shook his head and leaned against
Ronald's leg. "Dozens of cousins, six older
sisters, trained to kill on command, all the time
on the prowl, snarling at shadows—I'm not that
sort of weasel," he said quietly.

Ronald tugged at his ear. "That proves it,
Pa. Plenty of weasels have jobs. Just one
weasel has a bad name with the public, an
especially bad name with this bear." He
stepped back, and Warren fell on his face and
started to cry loudly.

"I should have known nobody could help.
I am a disaster, a house whose roof has caved
in, a brook who's flooded the fields."

"Stop carrying on, I'll keep thinking. Come
sit on my shoulder." Ronald helped Warren,
brushed the grass off him, and wiped his eyes.
"Massage my head, behind my ears, some of
my finest ideas come from that region."

Ronald glanced at his notes. "Item 159.
Engineer. Gardener, teacher, pilot, barber, did
I already say dentist?"

"I'm afraid of teeth."

"There's not much left."

"I used to like being a weasel. Sometimes
when you're chasing a mole, you crawl through
a hole, fight your way through dense grasses,

nose down to the scent, fur rippling. Most satisfactory."

"Anything else you like?"

"I do like to swim." Warren propelled his front paws as though the air was water. "Got any lakes around here?"

"With all the weasels in the world, I had to get the dumbest," Ronald screamed, and he ran back to the house.

"I wonder how Warren's mother keeps all her small weasels sorted out. Heard Warren scampering late into the night," Ma said.

"He was dusting my books," Ronald explained. "He's not lazy, you know." Ronald started to giggle. "When Pa said he had to cut the grass, Warren said, 'Give me the scissors and I'll cut it!'"

Ma laughed. "Scissors! He did say weasels aren't homebodies."

"See how I beat him every night—whatever game we play, I cream him. And he never sulks like Oliver."

"He is a nice soul," Ma agreed. "Good appetite, pleasant company."

Warren carefully brushed the dirt from his fur before going into the house. It was twilight. He missed his mother each evening, gathering the young weasels together, ready for the glorious night ahead. "Whiskers sharp, snout to the ground, *on, weasels, on on on!*"

Warren thought how slowly the bears moved. Probably all that toast and honey weighed them down.

When they were finishing supper, Pa said, "What a gigantic crop of vegetables we have out back. Wish Oliver was home—he does such a good job with the beans and peas."

"I have no time to harvest. I have my hands full." Ronald jerked his head toward Warren.

"Time for us bears to be in bed." Pa yawned. "And what are you going to do tonight, Warren?"

"I didn't finish counting the stars last night." Warren held up a piece of paper with smudged

dots covering half of it. "Ronald wants *all* of them counted."

"He's slow, Pa, but he's thorough. Look how clear Ursa Minor is." Ronald patted Warren's paw.

Warren waited next to Ronald's bed until the bear was ready for sleep. Then he handed Ronald his pillow.

"Aha! I'm on the track of something. Why don't you pick a few zucchini tonight? Ma makes delectable zucchini bread, light, moist, melts in your mouth."

"Good glorious day in the morning," Ma shouted.

"Warren, Warren, you frabjous weasel," Pa shouted.

Ronald dragged his half-asleep self into the kitchen. "Whatever is the matter? What has that foolish weasel done now?"

Ronald gasped.

Carrots were piled on all the chairs. Nuts in cups and glasses. A pyramid of zucchini almost as tall as Ma, peas, summer squash, snap beans, eggplants, onions, cucumbers tumbling out the front door, red peppers in pots and pans.

Ronald gasped.

Carrots were piled on all the chairs.

"Warren? Warren!" Ma began searching through the vegetables. "We have to find the little fellow. He might have got buried alive."

"We must be sure not to cook him with the eggplant," Pa said as he set the kettle to boil.

"Over here, behind the cabbages. What a night! Ronald, you don't mind if I take a nap in your bed? It will be all nice and warm." The tiny creature's head sagged forward.

Ronald was so happy, he felt as though he had been the one to surprise Ma and Pa. "I'll even tuck you in."

"What a wonderful weasel you are." Ma bent down and stroked Warren gently.

"I'm the one who's wonderful. It was my idea. I knew I was onto the scent. He is awake while we are asleep, didn't I say that last night?"

"We all knew that," Pa said.

"All this talk makes a bear hungry," Ma said, peeling an apple.

"Warren," Ronald proclaimed, "you can stay with us. You can be my personal assistant. You will guard my lab while I sleep. You can wash the dishes when it is my turn, hang up my clothes, take out the trash—"

"Just one minute, Ronald." Pa looked angry.

"OK, I'll wash the dishes," Ronald conceded. "I said it from the beginning, it's all how you look at a creature. Warren was the only one who thought he was a loser."

"I'll guard the woods, I'll be a hero, everyone will love me." Warren scampered and weaved among the vegetables and headed out the door. "Warren to the rescue." He ran toward the meadow. "Fire," he yelled.

"This is only a drill," Ronald shouted, following close behind.

"Hurray for Ronald, the smartest bear in the universe," they both shouted at once.

"Fire, murder, police," Warren shrieked.

"This is only a drill," Ronald yelled. Exhausted, he collapsed on the ground. When he looked up Warren was gone.

"You should be proud—that was one happy weasel sped out of here," Pa said.

"I taught him how to wash my test tubes—his tiny paws were great for that—I showed him where to hide during thunderstorms, he had never even seen a clock till he came here." Ronald brushed tears from his fur. "How could he leave now? Just when things were looking up?"

"Listen to that whistling—sounds like a crowd." Pa went to the window. "I think you have more clients, Ronald. Better put in a big batch of muffins, Ma."

"I am going out of business," Ronald said.

Warren appeared on the doorstep. "They're coming! We may set a weasel world record for long-distance running."

Ma squinted and looked toward the meadow. The tall grass seemed to be humming. Warren motioned to Ronald and sped off.

"They're coming!"

Warren shouted into a megaphone. "This is your cousin, Warren the Winner, speaking. Personal assistant to the smartest bear in the universe. Ronald will help all of you. No creature too small." Warren's voice was drowned out by the shouts of the other weasels.

"I have trouble falling asleep."

"I'm losing my fur."

"Lost the scent two or three years back."

"Do you have a piano? I'd like to learn to give concerts."

"Do you know geography?"

Warren's voice was drowned out by . . .

the shouts of the other weasels.

"Stop pushing and shoving, line up, *quiet*," Warren barked. "I have never seen weasels behave so rudely." He flicked two wrangling weasels with his tail. "Pay attention, or the smartest bear will send you away."

Ronald sat down under the blue oak and opened his notebook. Weasels were racing toward him from every direction.

"Why did you have to come from such a large family?" Ronald grinned and lifted Warren onto his shoulder.

"These are only my nearest relations. The woods are full of weasels. Wait till the word gets out."

"It will take us years to straighten out this mess," Ronald said happily. He licked the soft fold of Warren's ear. "*Me* all day, *you* all night."

THE END